BREAKOUTS

STRANGERS
ON A
PLANE

John Townsend

Rans⬤m

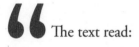 The text read:

Can U help me? In trouble. Need U 2 do something 4 me when we land. Don't turn round or look at me. Will explain later. Delete this. Todd.

Strangers on a Plane
by John Townsend

Published by Ransom Publishing Ltd.
Unit 7, Brocklands Farm, West Meon, Hampshire
GU32 1JN, UK
www.ransom.co.uk

ISBN   978 178591 147 7
First published in 2016

ONE

Cameras recorded every move. They panned across the airport concourse and zoomed in on passengers' faces – scanning for tell-tale signs. Lenses fixed on eyes and digitally analysed them. Any known terrorist would be matched against biometric data and instantly recognised.

Body-scanners, X-ray machines and internal bag searches examined below the surface. Hidden CCTV devices closely watched everyone in the departure lounge. Airport security software scrutinised body language and alerted guards to anyone acting suspiciously. All staff had been notified of the latest level of threat. Their computer screens flashed with the code: **S**. **S** for **SEVERE**.

A dangerous passenger was expected anytime soon. **RED ALERT**.

Officers in the security suite stared at banks of screens. They watched the boy in a denim jacket with rucksack as he strode across the departure lounge. He held a can of drink in one hand and a phone in the other. His image changed colour in response to the latest data. Level of threat = LOW. Safe.

A small window appeared on security screens:

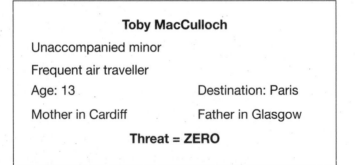

Toby MacCulloch

Unaccompanied minor

Frequent air traveller

Age: 13   Destination: Paris

Mother in Cardiff   Father in Glasgow

Threat = ZERO

The ring-pull snapped with a hiss and the can fizzed. A spurt of cola sprayed over Toby's jacket and he swore, as an officer read his lips on the screen and smiled. Checking his watch, Toby decided there was still enough time to sponge his stain-soaked sleeve, so he grabbed his rucksack and headed to the door marked *Gents' Washroom*. At a sink, he wetted a paper towel and rubbed his arm before holding it under the hand-dryer. He was glad to have the washroom to himself. All cubicles were empty, so he didn't have to worry about puzzled stares from strangers or where to put his rucksack. Even so, he slid it safely out of the way in a small space between the end cubicle and the wall. He didn't want his gift for Jodie (carefully bubble-wrapped inside) to get kicked and broken. When at last his sleeve was stain-free and dry, he went to get his rucksack, squeezing down the narrow space into the corner. As he stooped to grab it, he heard the door swing open behind him and a loud whisper at the sinks filled the washroom; urgent, foreign and assertive. 'It is OK – no one in here. Empty. We can talk. I talk – you listen.'

Knowing he couldn't be seen where he was, Toby

remained very still. It was best not to startle whoever was there, even though he felt awkward; hiding and crouched beside a toilet cubicle. He froze when the voice suddenly hissed aggressively. 'You got this far, so good. But I watch to make sure you don't mess up. If you do, I will strike. I will be following all the time. Three things you must know. One: don't let that bag out of your sight. Two: don't tip it on its side – it's safe as long as you don't break the tough lining. Three: don't forget the code and time is *two thirty* in French at Montblanc. Now go, quick. Remember cameras are everywhere. I'll give you half a minute before I follow you out. Make sure you don't look at me or show you know me. Get it wrong and you know what I will do. Go.'

Toby daren't move. If he gave himself away now, the man might turn even nastier. At the same time, he wanted to see what the speaker looked like and who he'd been talking to. After all, the conversation sounded a bit scary and suspicious. Should he report it? Yet as he began to think about it, Toby didn't really know how he could explain what he'd just witnessed. What exactly was there to tell anyone? Sounding nasty and making some sort of threat wasn't exactly a crime, was it? And it wasn't a proper conversation because the other person had said nothing. Toby had no idea how to describe either of them. The one who spoke sounded a bit French, but Toby still didn't have a clue what he looked like – so it was worth taking a quick peep. Or better still, if he could slowly stretch out his arm and take a photo on his phone, he could stay hidden. It was worth the risk. Holding his breath, Toby slowly raised his phone and pointed it towards the row of sinks. His finger touched the button and he paused, wondering what he might discover in the next few seconds.

*

Nothing. Toby stared at the image on his phone. All he could see was a fuzzy shadow in front of the door. When he enlarged it, the shape looked like the back of someone's head. He'd caught the man's silhouette as he was heading out through the door – a dark shape with broad shoulders and just a glint of an ear cuff at the top of his left ear.

Toby was in two minds what to do. Should he tell someone he was hiding in the toilets and happened to overhear a strange man sounding menacing? That just seemed too weird. Although there was nothing really criminal in what the man had said, Toby couldn't help feeling there was something worrying or dangerous about him. Something sinister. But who would listen to the bizarre hunch of a 13 year-old who lurked in public toilets? Maybe it would be best if he forgot the whole thing.

By the time Toby emerged from his hiding place, a cleaner in orange overalls was mopping the floor. He wore earphones and was whistling loudly, totally oblivious to Toby creeping out past him and returning hurriedly to the busy departure lounge … and then on to Paris.

TWO

An air steward in royal blue waistcoat and crimson tie bustled across the departure lounge. 'Hi, Toby. You've got me again. You okay?'

Toby glanced up from his phone. 'Hi, Gavin. Yeah – good, thanks. Dad wasn't too grumpy this time. He actually got me here without breaking the speed limit and jumping the lights.'

The steward scrolled through his iPad. 'You've not done this flight before – why Paris?'

'They actually let me on the school Disneyland Paris trip! First time ever. I'm joining them there. I had to be here this weekend for my Gran's 70th. I wouldn't have missed that – my Gran's epic. Amazingly, my school's letting me meet them at Paris Airport – I'm well-chuffed. Life just keeps getting better.'

'Don't bank on it, sunshine. I don't envy you getting through Paris today. It'll be manic – they're holding a World Summit Assembly there. Security will be mega. Please reassure me you're not a terrorist.'

Toby laughed, but wondered if it might be best to mention the man in the washroom.

'Talking of security, I'm a bit concerned about a guy I overheard just now in the loos. I know it sounds weird but I was out of sight and couldn't see his face, but he was saying something about a bag and stuff. Sort of threatening someone. Too thuggy for my liking.'

Gavin frowned. 'Did he have a weapon or anything? Violent, was he? Drunk maybe? I need a bit more info to flag up an SSA. That's a Significant Security Alert. I'll have to download the forms.'

'No, none of that – it's just that I felt really uneasy. Something wasn't right.'

'Hmm, not a lot to go on. You're welcome to make a statement if you like.' Gavin looked at his watch. 'Trouble is, it'll take time and you'll miss this flight.'

Toby sighed, 'In that case, I'll forget it. It's probably not worth the fuss. How long till take-off? Will it be on time?'

Gavin ticked boxes on his iPad and looked at the departures screen. 'Yep. All ticker-te-boo. I'll take you through to the plane in about five mins – ahead of the crowd. I've got two of you to look after on this flight.' He looked back at his iPad. 'A boy called Todd. I've never seen him before. Older than you by a couple of years. He ought to be here by now. I just hope he's not one of the stroppy lads I get sometimes. If only all my U.M.s were perfect little angels like you, Toby! In my experience, U.M. doesn't just stand for 'Unaccompanied Minor' but 'Utterly Mental'. I had to manage a teenage girl yesterday who had a fit of the screaming abdabs over Dusseldorf.'

'In that case, I'll try not to self-combust over Doncaster!' Toby grinned.

Gavin was absorbed in checking details on his iPad. 'Please don't. Think of the paperwork. I've got Todd's mobile number here. I'd better give him a call, I reckon. We don't want him lost in the maze of corridors round here.'

'There's lots of security guards about today. More than normal,' Toby said casually, as he leant back in his seat while tapping at his phone.

Gavin looked into the distance, scanning a queue at the cafe. 'There's been a few incidents lately. Some nutters about, it seems.'

Toby couldn't help wondering if Gavin was referring to him and his hunch in the washroom. In the cold light of day, it did seem to be a fuss over nothing. He swiftly put it to the back of his mind and thought about meeting up with Jodie and school friends in Paris in a couple of hours. That would be so awesome. He smiled, thinking of his crazy present for her in his rucksack.

It was now Gavin who appeared concerned. 'Look, I'll just pop to the office and sort out Todd. I'll be back in a couple of ticks,' he said, dashing off to a door marked PRIVATE with a fingerprint lock.

Toby returned to the latest texts on his phone, but was suddenly aware of a figure standing nearby. It was someone also engrossed in a phone – a tall lad in really smart jeans, a burgundy hoodie with designer label and top-of-the-range white trainers. His thick black hair was in neat cornrows and his eyebrows were shaved with tiny zigzags. As he stooped to open a navy blue canvas Lacoste shoulder bag at his feet, he turned and looked directly at Toby. Despite his super-cool manner and stylish appearance, his dark eyes told another story. Toby could tell he was terrified.

'Are you Todd, by any chance?' Toby asked.

The boy stared, open-mouthed, but for some seconds seemed frozen and unable to speak. 'How do you know me? Who are you? I've never seen you.'

'It's okay,' Toby began, 'I just assumed you must be the guy the steward was looking for. Gavin told me I wasn't the only kid flying alone, but someone called Todd was also on the flight and by himself. Gavin's in the office and … '

Before he could finish speaking, the boy's phone bleeped. He snatched at it and spoke with a definite edge to his voice. 'Yeah. Okay. Yeah.'

After putting the phone in his pocket, he paused, took a deep breath as if deliberately trying to calm himself, and stepped towards Toby with his hand outstretched. 'Sorry. Things have been a bit tense. I'm Todd. Glad to meet you. That was our steward making sure I hadn't been kidnapped.' He gripped Toby's hand and shook it firmly. He beamed a genuine smile.

'So who are you?' he asked.

'I'm Toby. I fly from here a lot. First time to Paris, though. My dad lives here, so I come up for the odd weekend and in the holidays. I love flying, do you?'

'Not much. The thing is … '

Before he could say any more, Gavin returned in a fluster. 'Come on, you guys – I've got to get you aboard the plane pronto. How are you doing, Todd? Hey, I love your trainers! Can you just check your details on my list for me?' He handed Todd the iPad. 'While you're doing that I need to collect my stuff and I'll meet you both at the gate in thirty secs … '

A camera lens zoomed in. It watched Todd flick through details on an iPad while Toby turned to put his phone in his rucksack. Only the camera saw Todd pull back his left sleeve and scribble a number on it. By the time Toby turned back, the pen was back in Todd's pocket and his sleeve covered the scrawled digits. The camera processed the image and software analysed the information. Screens in the security suite showed a tiny window for just a few seconds:

Todd Boro
Unaccompanied minor
First-time air traveller
Age: 15
Trainee footballer
Threat = UNKNOWN

The camera moved on. Nothing suspicious. After all, it's not a crime to record a phone number … least of all from a fellow unaccompanied minor.

The two boys moved to the departure gate, reunited Gavin with his iPad, then walked with him towards the plane waiting somewhere outside on the tarmac.

THREE

'Great – I've got a seat by the window!' Toby pushed his rucksack into the overhead locker and looked around at the sea of empty blue seats. Gavin consulted his iPad yet again. 'Make yourselves comfy and I'll bring you both a drink after take-off. Your seat is second from the back, Todd. Excuse me while I go and check the snacks trolley.' He hurried to the front of the plane, leaving Toby looking down at the wing from his window.

'I just love watching the wing-flaps on take-off and seeing the runway fall away below us.' Toby assumed

Todd was somewhere down the plane, but suddenly his face was right by his ear. 'Hey, Toby – I need to talk to you. I haven't got long. I'm in a bit of trouble and … ' he pulled away suddenly and tried to whistle nonchalantly as another steward arrived and the first of the passengers began climbing the steps.

'I'll talk later.' Todd grunted awkwardly and disappeared to the back of the plane as a little old lady, in stylish olive green coat with matching gloves and handbag, walked elegantly along the aisle, took out her reading glasses to check her ticket and promptly sat beside Toby. She had coiffured white hair and a face like a china doll's, with delicately rouged cheeks.

'Are you all by yourself, dear?' she smiled at Toby. Her voice was husky, a smoker's voice, with a strong French accent. Toby could smell expensive perfume and more than a hint of tobacco smoke.

'Yes,' he smiled back, 'The steward is keeping his eye on me – so don't worry. I'm properly house-trained.'

The woman giggled. 'How frightfully funny. I don't mind kids. I was a teacher once, so I can deal with excitable teenagers. Do you like Paris? I love Paris.'

'I've never been before. I'm going to Disneyland Paris.'

'How exciting,' she said. 'I wish I was your age again. I live in Scotland but I'm going to my grandson's wedding. Would you like a mint?' She rummaged in her handbag while Toby watched the remaining passengers enter the plane. The last was a thick-set man in dark glasses and black leather coat, who was having something of an agitated conversation with Gavin at the door.

'I'll let you into a little secret,' the woman said with a wink. 'I'm glad I've got a nice young man beside me when we take off. I get a little nervous, you see.'

'Don't worry, I'll look after you. My gran says I'm good with older ladies. My gran is totally epic.'

The woman chuckled all through Gavin's safety talk about what to do in the event of a 'water landing'. She wheezed in a loud whisper, 'In the event of a water landing, you'll have to get me a dirty great brandy!'

She gasped at a sudden startling noise from Toby's phone. He'd downloaded a ringtone called 'piano falling' which usually made people laugh, but now heads turned disapprovingly, just as Gavin announced pointedly that all phones had to be turned to 'aircraft mode'.

'Sorry about that,' Toby muttered sheepishly, before looking at the text he'd just received. He was astounded to see it was from Todd.

> Toby, Can U help me? In trouble. Need U 2 do
> something 4 me when we land. Don't turn round or
> look at me. Will explain later. Delete this. Todd

As the plane began moving towards the runway, Toby pressed his face against the window. He wanted to see everything, even though his mind was now distracted by

Todd's strange message. Suddenly the engines roared, the seats shook and the plane rumbled down the runway – faster and faster. Thrust back into his seat, Toby watched the world flash past outside and begin to fall away as they climbed steeply above the rooftops.

'Wow – just feel the power!'

The woman beside him had her eyes shut and her hands gripped the armrests. Toby leaned towards her, just as his ears popped, and whispered, 'You can relax now. We're in the air. Less than two hours and we'll be landing. That's the best bit of all.'

'Not if it's a water landing.' She opened one eye and smiled. 'You are very sweet, my dear. What is your name?'

'Toby. My teacher calls me Tobias – which I loathe.'

She touched his hand. 'Then I shall only call you Toby. My name is Germaine – but you will probably call me "that batty old woman".'

She chuckled again, before offering him another mint. By the time they were skimming through the clouds, she was talking non-stop about her family, Paris and how the airport would be 'bursting at the seams with all those world leaders jetting in for some big conference on terrorism.'

Toby re-read the text from Todd, stored his number, then deleted the message. He looked out of the window into dark clouds, still lost in his thoughts. Whatever was going on with Todd? He couldn't forget the look of fear in his eyes when they first met. He wanted to turn round and give him a reassuring thumbs-up, but the command 'don't look at me' must have been for a reason. But why? Whatever might be going on, Toby was determined to get to the bottom of it.

He thought back to the incident in the washroom. Scrolling through his photos, he looked again at the fuzzy image of the man leaving through the door. The back of his head was just a silhouette but Toby enlarged the left ear to maximum. There seemed to be a black rim, like the earpiece of a pair of glasses. The ear cuff, although blurry, shone silver. He examined it very closely and could just make out what looked like the shape of a tiny face with eyes and a mouth. 'Blimey,' he said aloud, 'it's a silver skull!'

In that instant the whole plane juddered, as lightning crackled through the angry sky. A blinding streak of jagged light ripped through the clouds, flashed in Toby's eyes and the woman beside him screamed.

FOUR

The pilot announced the storm had finally passed and the plane would be landing in a few minutes, just as Toby peered down on the sprawl of Paris emerging below the clouds. The woman next to him stopped whimpering, gripped her armrests once more and crunched yet another mint as the plane banked steeply. Above the drone of the descending undercarriage, Toby gave a running commentary on the moving wing-flaps and the position of the runway rising towards them.

'Spare me the details, Toby,' she said. 'Just let me

know when we've landed so I can open my eyes.'

After a jolt and the screech of tyres, followed by a 'yes' from Toby, the plane juddered as the engines thundered into reverse thrust.

'We're slowing down and heading towards the terminal. We're safe and sound,' Toby announced, 'so you can open your eyes now and glimpse the wonder of Charles de Gaulle Airport. And what's more, you're still in one piece, Germaine. Welcome to Paris. Epic!'

She placed her hand on his. 'Toby, you've been wonderful. If I were seventy years younger I would fall in love with you.' She giggled as Gavin appeared beside them. 'I'll take you *U.M.s* off first and deliver you to your guardians, before I head off to Berlin. It's all go, eh?'

'It's been great flying with you, Germaine. You remind me of my Gran. She's totally epic, too.' Toby shook her hand and squeezed past her to collect his rucksack from the locker. It was only then that he glanced back to look for Todd. All passengers were unclipping seatbelts and standing, as Todd made his way down the plane. Only one passenger remained seated and still – the man in dark glasses and leather coat. He was chewing gum vigorously and dabbing at his sweaty forehead with a handkerchief. He seemed more interested in watching others than collecting his hand luggage. In fact, despite his dark glasses, his eyes seemed to be fixed on Todd and Toby as they were being led off the plane ahead of everyone else.

As soon as they began descending the steps, Todd grabbed Toby's elbow.

'Did you get my text?'

'Yeah,' Toby said. 'What's up?'

'If anything happens to me. If I don't make it … there's a guy on the plane – dark glasses, leather coat. Get a photo of him and tell security it was him.'

Gavin was already several steps ahead and striding

onto the ramp into the airport building, beyond earshot.

Todd whispered, 'Walk a bit slower and listen, but look as if you're not. He'll be watching us from the plane. I've got to make him think I'm carrying out his instructions. If not, they'll get me. I've got to deliver this bag in … ' he looked at his watch. 'In exactly fifteen minutes.'

'So what's the problem?' Toby asked. 'I mean, why not just do as he wants?'

'I'm sure this bag has got something dangerous in it. Don't ask me what exactly. It might be something for making a bomb. I can tell it's a liquid. They got me to bring it so police won't be able to follow the trail and trace the real terrorists. I'm sure that's who they are. I reckon one of them will assemble some kind of explosive from what I deliver. This airport must be the target.'

Toby stopped walking. 'What? That can't happen! They can't involve innocent kids, surely?'

'Kids like us on our own don't get searched like adults. They knew I'd get the bag through security. But if I tell anyone or mess up, they'll get me. They said so. And my kid brother. He arrived here yesterday with our real luggage and he should be here to meet me. We're doing football camp at Paris Football Academy. At first I thought these guys were genuine talent scouts. They gave us smart clothes and got us signed up here for training. But there's something else going on. We're just their carriers to get stuff through security. No one suspects a kid going to football camp of carrying bad stuff. It's sealed inside this bag. So now you know in case anything terrible happens.'

Toby couldn't help staring at the innocent-looking Lacoste shoulder bag. 'But how come scanners and X-rays didn't detect that stuff?'

'Security staff collected me at the check-in desk, confirmed my ID and led me straight through. They were more interested in asking me about football and my trial for Spurs. I only had to take off my trainers and empty my pockets, but they didn't bother with anything else because I'm an unaccompanied minor who happens to be a junior premier footballer. They only opened the bag and took a quick peep inside. I didn't know till later I was carrying something secret. The guy on the plane told me stuff is hidden in the lining.'

By now Gavin was approaching the desk where he was about to hand over his charges for collection. Toby looked over his shoulder to check if the other passengers from their flight had entered the building yet. 'That guy with dark glasses,' he asked, 'did he have an ear cuff like a silver skull?'

'Yeah, that's him. He's some kind of evil fanatic. He told me he and his followers want revenge and make the world tremble. He's a nutter, for sure – but a scary and determined one.'

'I was in the washroom and heard him telling you not to let the bag out of your sight or tip it on its side. Also something about a code time and Montblanc. I knew something bad was going on. I wish I'd done something about it now.'

Gavin pointed at a desk marked *Enquêtes Bureau*.

'Just wait here, lads and I'll get you sorted. This place is heaving with security. I've never seen so many armed guards patrolling here. It looks like the VIP lounge is packed with top international politicians.'

Todd clutched the bag in his arms. 'I can't go ahead with this. I'll have to take the risk.' He coolly walked past Toby and Gavin to speak to a woman at the desk. 'Excusez moi, parlez vous anglais?'

'Yes,' the woman smiled, 'I speak English. Can I help you?'

'I hope so,' Todd said calmly. 'There's something I need to tell you.'

Suddenly a hand grabbed his shoulder and a voice groaned, 'You've got to help me,' before a body slid to the floor with a sigh.

FIVE

Cameras recorded every move. They panned across the airport and zoomed in on passengers' faces.

Officers in the security suite stared at banks of monitors, focussing on the boy in a denim jacket with rucksack as he lay sprawled on the floor by the enquiries desk.

A small window appeared on security screens:

```
Mineurs non accompagnés
            Toby MacCulloch
Nationalité Britannique
L'âge de 13 ans
Destination: Paris
        Menace de sécurité = ZÉRO
```

'I'm ill,' Toby spluttered. 'I'm going to be sick. Can you get me to a medical room quickly, Todd?'

Gavin looked down in horror at the annoying interruption to his tight schedule. 'Er, don't worry, Toby – I'll sort you out. Try not to be sick right here, eh?' He glanced desperately at the woman behind the desk. 'Is there somewhere? Just a quiet room to sort him out with a bucket or something?'

She, too, peered down with a look of revulsion at the gurgling noises on the floor. She raised an arm and pointed. 'Over there. Door code is the date.'

Todd hesitated. He was desperate to explain everything to her, unload all his worries and then deal with the circumstances. But the hands grabbing at his white trainers seemed even more desperate. He reached down and said, 'Okay, Toby – let me pull you up and I'll help you over to the MI room.'

With Gavin holding one arm and Todd the other, they slid Toby across the floor to a locked door down a side corridor with the sign *Salle Médicale*. Gavin tapped in the digits of the date onto the keypad and the door buzzed open. A bare white room inside had grey plastic chairs and a stretcher with a red blanket. Slouching on a chair with his head in his hands, Toby groaned, 'Any chance of some water?'

'I'll go and find you a cup or something.' Todd was about to leave when Toby called him back.

'No, please stay, Todd. Gavin will know where to look – and to find an icepack for my head. Can you, Gavin?'

'Er yeah, okay – sure. Hold on … ' As Gavin hurried from the room, Toby immediately sprang to life.

'Todd, listen to me. I'm fine. I wanted to stop you reporting all that stuff just then. There was a scary-looking woman in a long purple shawl watching you like a hawk and trying to listen. I reckon it's safer for you to go along with what that skull guy and his gang want a bit longer. If you raise the alarm now, this place will go crazy and in all the chaos, the bad guys will scatter. Upset them now and you and your brother will be instant targets. But keep them happy a bit longer and we might be able to fool them. You're scared of these nutters, right? But the safest place for you right now is here where there are cameras and massive security everywhere. But once they know you've reported them and you're out there in a strange city, they'll soon hunt you down. Trust me, Todd, I've got an idea to catch them all red-handed before they can run to ground like the cowards they are. And I reckon anyone who gets innocent kids to do their risky dirty work are the biggest cowards of all.'

'I kind of get your point, Toby – but what's the plan?' Todd kept looking at the door in case Gavin returned. 'Let's ask Gavin what he thinks.'

Toby shook his head. 'He'll just panic and blurt everything to the world. One hint that their plot is threatened, the terrorists will run for it, only to strike again, after they've dealt with you. So why not carry on as normal? If you leave that bag where you were told, we'll get to see who collects it and what they do. I'll take pictures of the bad guys, hand over the evidence and security will nab the lot of them before they do any harm. Then they'll get locked up – so you and your brother will never be bothered by them again. Does that make sense?'

Before he could get a reply, Toby threw himself on the stretcher with a pathetic whimper, just as Gavin swept in with a glass of water and an icepack. 'Here, Toby – pop this ice on your head and sip this water. How are you feeling?'

'I think it was the food I ate on the plane,' Toby mumbled.

Gavin looked horrified. 'I hope not. Oh, by the way, Todd – the woman at the desk asked to see you. Just a quick message.'

Todd picked up his bag. 'Then I'd better go see what she wants.'

'You can leave your bag here with us. I'll look after it,' Gavin said, holding the glass of water to Toby's lips.

'I'm not supposed to let it out of my sight, so you'd better guard it with your life!' Todd carefully placed it under a chair and turned to give Toby a quick smile before leaving the room.

'It's okay, Gavin – you can take the icepack off my head now before I catch hyperthermia. I think it's done the trick as I'm feeling a bit better.'

'That's good,' Gavin kept looking at his watch, 'as I really need to get going. Is it okay if I hand you over to another member of staff who'll take you to meet your teacher when you feel ready?'

'I'll never feel ready to meet the dreaded Mrs Porter,' Toby laughed. 'For some reason she just doesn't like me. She's forever accusing me of telling lies or being as irritating as a lump of grit in her shoe. I just hope she'll be in a good mood today. At least Jodie will be with her to keep the peace. In fact, she should be somewhere nearby – can she come in here to see me?'

'You'll have to wait till we get to the arrivals area. She's not allowed in this zone as it's only for passengers who've cleared security. This is known as the safe sector. Look, it's been great meeting you again, Toby – but I've got to dash. I'll send in one of my colleagues to sort you out and take you to see Jodie. I'm sure you'll soon be feeling tip-top – especially when you get to Disneyland. Have fun.'

He shook Toby's hand, looked at his watch again and dashed from the room – which immediately filled with the deafening sound of a crashing piano falling from a great height. Toby grabbed his phone and read the text with absolute horror. It was from Todd:

HELP – THEY'VE GOT ME.

SIX

Toby ran from the medical room and through the crowds in the duty free mall. He was jostled and elbowed as he desperately searched for any sign of Todd, whose text screamed in Toby's head: *They've got me*.

But who and where? The only way Toby could help now was to tell security and raise the alarm. It was time to warn of a sinister plot unfolding around them. He pushed through the queue at the enquiries desk and tried to attract the attention of the woman they'd seen earlier. She didn't seem pleased to see him.

'There is a queue – you've pushed in. If you are now

better, just wait there and a member of staff will take you to your school teacher shortly.'

'No, it's not that,' Toby began in an urgent whisper, trying not to startle others around him. 'Someone's kidnapped the boy I was with. He's in danger. There are terrorists here – right now. They're probably watching me, as well. So I'll be next on their hit list. You must tell security immediately.'

The woman stared at him with a look of total disbelief and increasing anger.

'Stop such nonsense instantly. You're one of those annoying children who just wants to be the centre of attention, aren't you? I wasn't convinced you were really ill just then. It was all an act to make a fuss. You seem perfectly fine to me so sit over there and wait to be taken to your teacher – who has just phoned through to ask where you are. She did warn that you have an over-active imagination. "Very bright but irritating", she said. I question the 'bright'.'

He thumped the desk and raised his voice, as all heads turned. 'This has got nothing to do with imagination. Listen to me. Todd has been kidnapped and I've just got a text from him asking for help. He was carrying something in his bag for a thuggy Frenchman on the plane. Something dangerous – a bomb, maybe … '

The woman bristled, her eyes raged and her finger reached for a button under the desk. 'Don't you dare say such things here. That's outrageous nonsense. Your friend Todd was collected from right here just minutes ago. His auntie was thrilled to meet him and take him off on a sight-seeing trip.'

'That can't be true,' Toby spluttered. 'She must have been one of the gang. He's now in terrible danger – and we could be, too.'

She ignored him and hissed in a dangerously soft voice, through clenched teeth, 'You are about to be escorted from the premises. Just go and grow up.'

'I can prove Todd was kidnapped,' he continued,

even more frustrated and desperately searching his pockets. 'I can show you his text. Ah, I must have left my phone in the medical room. But hey, come and take a look in Todd's bag and you'll see what I'm talking about. You'll find something dangerous inside. Security must act fast to stop the big guy with sunglasses on the plane who's about to commit some kind of terror attack – I just know I'm right. You've got to believe me.'

A security guard appeared at his side and there followed a gabbled conversation between him and the woman, whose annoyance was just as obvious in French. From the way they spoke and stared at him aggressively, he could tell this was going from bad to worse. He tried to make sense of the babbling string of disjointed words: *Sac à bandoulière … les explosives … message texte … menace terroriste … stupide d'imagination … idiot anglais …*

Toby interrupted, 'Just let me show him the evidence in the medical room.'

More gabbling: *Salle medical … éléments de prevue … gardez le garçon calme.*

The guard sneered and snapped, 'Come. Show.' He gabbled into a mouthpiece attached to his ear and strode towards the medical room. At the door, he grunted and beckoned Toby inside. 'Come. Show.'

Rushing over to his rucksack lying on the stretcher, Toby fumbled inside. 'I'll show you the text from Todd. My phone is in here … somewhere.'

He rummaged in every pocket and frantically unzipped each compartment.

'It should be in here. Really – my phone has gone. Someone has taken it.'

The guard said nothing but stood with legs astride, folding his arms and staring with stone-cold eyes. 'Les explosives?' he scoffed.

'Todd's bag is under the chair. I don't know what's in it but … ' Toby froze and stared in disbelief at the empty space under the chair. He searched all corners of the room and threw the blanket on the floor.

'It was here, Honest. It's gone. They've taken it.'

The guard stepped forward and barked, 'Go'. His impatient command filled the small room and crashed against the walls like a gunshot.

Toby's head was in a whirl. A seed of doubt began to sprout in his mind. What if he'd got it all wrong? Maybe his imagination had played tricks. Maybe he should just go quietly and forget all about it. But what if Todd was in real danger? He felt a hand grip his shoulder as the guard dragged him from the room.

'Get out. Go.'

Feeling completely humiliated and baffled, Toby strapped on his rucksack and sighed feebly as the door to the medical room was slammed shut behind him. The guard was giving a sneering commentary into his mouthpiece and Toby was certain he heard the words *'pathétique'* and *'imbécile'*.

Looking out across the vast concourse swarming

with people, all on the move and oblivious to any danger, Toby felt more determined than ever to follow his instinct. He'd have to act alone. Whoever had taken his phone and Todd's bag couldn't be far away. Glancing along one of the shopping malls, he was sure he glimpsed the head and shoulders of the man in dark glasses. There was no time to lose.

Just as the guard tugged at Toby's elbow to lead him firmly back to the desk and presumably to be frogmarched from the airport, he twisted round, yanked himself free and ran. He hurtled down a causeway through the milling crowd, with the screaming guard close behind.

People scattered as he darted through them, round a corner past an escalator, down a precinct between jewellers' shops and luggage boutiques, straight across a glitzy island selling lottery tickets from a shiny red sports car, then he dodged between tables at an open cafe. Hurling himself along a moving walkway, he looked back at the shouts behind him. The guard clattered through cafe tables, collided with a waiter balancing a tray and sprawled on the floor among smashing cups. Toby ran on, cutting through an internet lounge 'Espace Multimedia' and on past Starbucks. Stopping momentarily to see where the man in dark glasses had gone, he heard a familiar voice behind him.

'Would you like a drink, Toby? It looks like you need a rest.'

The old woman from the plane was smiling at him. 'Are you in a hurry by any chance?'

'Germaine!' Toby gasped. 'Er, I'm in a spot of bother right now.'

'Then you'd better come for a little chat. I'd love a coffee. How about right there?' She pointed across the thoroughfare to Caffè Ritazza, just as raised voices echoed behind them, getting closer all the time. Toby looked back at the commotion and saw more guards running in all directions. 'Fine,' he said. He took her arm and led her briskly through the door.

As soon as they were seated, Toby blurted, 'Those guards are after me.'

She looked at him with a sparkle in her eye. 'How exciting. I'm sure you haven't done anything too terrible. To be honest, I thought it might be me they're after. I just bought a scarf in Montblanc and nearly walked out without paying for it. It wasn't my fault as they were closing in rather a rush.'

Toby's thoughts were elsewhere and only one of her words cut through his churning mind. 'Did you say Montblanc?' He tried desperately to remember why that particular word meant something among all the other confusing thoughts swirling around his head. His brain flashed back to the conversation he'd overhead in the washroom before the flight. An urgent whisper with a strong French accent had insisted, 'Don't forget the code and time is *two thirty* in French at Montblanc.'

'Yes, dear. It's the clothes boutique just here – next to the posh VIP lounge full of politicians. I've already spotted a couple of famous ones.'

Toby stood up. 'That's where something's about to happen. I just know it. I need to go to Montblanc.'

'I told you, they're now closed. They won't let you in.'

'They will if I know the code. *Two thirty* in French. What's *two thirty* in French?'

'Toby, you're not making much sense.' She looked at her watch. 'But two thirty is in ten minutes, which in French is *deux heures et demie*.'

'Then I'd better do something quick,' he said, undoing his rucksack. 'I reckon that whatever's going to happen – it will be at two thirty exactly.'

He took a small box from his rucksack with bubble-wrap inside. 'I bought this as a laugh for Jodie as she can never get up in the mornings. It's an alarm clock that fires a flying saucer with a super-loud siren. I'm going to set it for two thirty. I'll only let it go off if there really is something scary going on. Can you be outside

Montblanc and if you hear it, tell security to come and get me.'

She gave him a quizzical glance before looking past him through the window. 'Talking of alarms – I don't want to alarm you, Toby, but there are quite a lot of armed guards out there. They're obviously looking for someone. I wonder if it might be someone in a denim jacket.' She smiled and winked knowingly.

Keeping his back to the window, Toby quickly removed his jacket. 'Can I ask another big favour, Germaine? It could make all the difference.'

'It will be my pleasure. I think I know what you want. I'll trust you because you were so kind to me earlier and I think this is very exciting. I'm sure you will explain everything later, but I haven't had such fun for years. I know you're a nice boy really, Toby. In fact, I would go as far to say I think you're totally epic!'

She gave a chuckle as she removed her coat and handed it to him. 'The scarf is in the pocket,' she whispered secretively. 'I hope it suits you. I'll be there in ten minutes when you've done whatever you need to do – and I wish you the very best of luck.'

SEVEN

Cameras were watching. They panned across the bustling crowds and zoomed in on passengers' faces. Officers in the security suite stared at banks of screens. Software was hurriedly adjusted to search for a boy of medium build in a denim jacket with rucksack. Anyone resembling his image was instantly targeted and his movements monitored. Instructions from the control room crackled through guards' earpieces on all floors of the airport. Any suspect would be swiftly removed for interrogation.

The plump figure in long olive-green coat and floral headscarf moved towards the Montblanc Boutique. Neither cameras nor the watching security guards took much notice. With rucksack strapped to his front under Germaine's coat, Toby shuffled along with bent back and bowed head. No one seemed to notice his trainers and brightly striped socks below rolled-up jeans.

A young woman was dressing a mannequin in glamorous evening wear in the window of Montblanc. Finding the door locked, Toby tapped on the glass. The woman shook her head but looked more closely as he mouthed, 'Deux heures et demie.'

She took pins from her mouth and, bare-footed, stepped from the window. 'Okay. Un moment.'

The door opened in a rattle of keys, Toby stepped inside and the woman hurriedly returned to her display with an abrupt, 'Aidez-vous vous-même.'

The shop was in semi-darkness; just racks of clothes and not a soul in sight. The only sound came from distant voices drifting in through air vents, interrupted by occasional echoing flight announcements. Toby crept by changing rooms and past dresses hanging like phantoms in the eerie stillness. Removing the coat and scarf, he listened to a hum of conversation through the wall in the VIP lounge next door. As silently as he could, he pulled back a curtain in the corner and stepped into a store room with an aluminium ladder leading up through a hatch in the ceiling from where he heard muffled shuffles and scrapes. Very gingerly, he placed his foot on the bottom rung and slowly began to climb.

The ladder creaked as he poked his head up into the vast darkness above the suspended ceiling tiles. Before his eyes could adjust to the gloom, a torch flashed in his face and a hand grabbed his throat. Dragged by his neck, Toby was hurled up onto wooden boards where he lay sprawled, blinking up at a low ceiling a metre above him, where a single light and a bag were suspended. It was a bag he recognised; navy blue with the Lacoste logo. Unable to struggle free from the weight of someone kneeling on his chest, Toby soon lay bound and gagged, his rucksack thrown to one side and its contents strewn all over.

'It's that kid from the plane,' he heard a familiar gruff voice grunt: urgent, foreign and assertive. 'I told you he could be trouble. But not any more.'

No dark glasses or silver ear-cuff were visible now. The two figures looking down at Toby were covered in white overalls and facemasks, wearing goggles, surgical gloves and shoe covers, just like CSI officers. One was short and slim, the other was large with thick-set shoulders. He was the one who spoke. 'It's the kid I took the phone from. Todd must have told him we'd be here.' The man spoke directly at Toby next. 'Just as well we got rid of Todd when we did. I sensed he might squeal under pressure. At least he got the bag through security – before I had him drugged and bundled in the back of a van in the car park, ready for disposal. You will be dispatched even sooner. Like now.'

He turned to the other white figure and said, 'Get a vial and I'll kill him here.'

Toby squinted up at Todd's bag hanging above him, from which dangled a tube that led into a ventilation duct. Could that really be a bomb, he wondered.

As if reading his mind, the man stooped to speak softly in Toby's ear.

'In a few minutes I will fulfil my dream. At half past two the VIP lounge will be packed with the most powerful people in the world. The very men and women I despise. That is when we release the deadly liquid from that bag. Sarin is one of the most toxic substances on the planet. It will dribble into the ventilation system where it will quickly evaporate. Within minutes a deadly cloud of sarin gas will drift down through the lounge next door. There will be no survivors.'

Toby blinked up at the other figure who held a tiny glass vial with what looked like a drop of water inside.

'My friend here has one job to do first,' the man went on, 'She will remove the stopper from that vial and drip sarin onto your skin. Within seconds you will be dead.

By the time the security guards discover you and the bodies next door, we will have made our escape and be far away. I will go down in history as the man who destroyed democracy. Such is my genius.'

Holding the vial delicately between finger and thumb of her gloved right hand, the ghostly figure stepped towards Toby and raised the deadly liquid above his face. But before she could remove the stopper, a sudden explosion of ear-splitting squeals ripped through them. A screaming siren filled the whole space and bounced off the ceiling with a piercing wail. From his rucksack, Toby saw the alarm clock flashing as it shot out a spinning disc that sliced through the air with a screech – slamming into the woman's hand. The vial slipped from her grasp, fell and rolled across the floor, as she scrambled to retrieve it. Crawling across a narrow path of floorboards, she reached over to the alarm clock in an attempt to quieten its deafening scream. Her knee crunched on the vial and she gasped as a glass splinter pierced her skin. It wasn't the spot of blood on the knee of her white overall that made her scream – but the smear of sarin seeping into the wound. She staggered forward, just as shouts from security guards and their clambering boots on the ladder rose from below.

Ear-cuff man rushed towards the hanging bag, groping to release the liquid. Before he could turn the tiny tap, he was rugby-tackled to the ground. Kicking out and yelling, he broke away and scuttled into the darkness beyond – just as the woman slumped forward with a gurgling groan. She rolled off the boards and crashed through the flimsy floor to the room below – landing at the feet of a president sipping a cup of tea on a sofa.

Holding his breath and with his shirt pulled up over his mouth, Toby shouted through the hole beside him – down to the lounge below. 'Get out quick. Don't breath in!'

The room emptied in seconds ... with no gas released or inhaled. The only casualty, apart from a poisoned terrorist lying rigid in the VIP lounge, was a broken digestive biscuit on the floor.

An expensive one at that.

EIGHT

Cameras recorded every move. They panned across the airport concourses and car parks, zooming in on any suspect likely to be behind the recent attack. Within minutes, a whole section of the airport was evacuated and sealed off. Patrols set up road blocks around the airport perimeter. After a warning from Toby, police marksmen swiftly surrounded a white van driven by a woman in a purple shawl. She and her accomplices were arrested after a noisy struggle, but their drowsy prisoner in the back was calmly unstrapped and released. Todd cheered as he walked free – led back to find Toby.

Security staff in facemasks and police with tasers were soon making a thorough search for anyone hiding in the concealed roof space above the deserted VIP lounge. Make-shift searchlights were unable to reach into the darkest nooks and crannies, where at least one suspect was thought to be lying low.

As Toby was led away to safety, he said to a policewoman, 'Just an idea – but can I make a phone call? I might be able to find the guy who's hiding.'

With a shrug, she reluctantly handed him a phone. He tapped in his number and suddenly the unmistakable noise of a falling piano burst from the darkest corner in the roof space. Lights spun round onto a white figure breaking out from the shadows, frantically fumbling to switch off the phone blaring in his pocket. A taser fired in an instant and he fell with a crackling scream, crashing through to the men's washroom below in a shower of smashed tiles. He landed with a thud and was immediately sat on by a rugby-scrum of armed officers. Thrashing and writhing, he swore as his face was pressed in a nasty puddle on the floor and, when a small silver skull rolled across tiles into the urinal, he lifted his head and muttered, 'Comment je déteste ce gosse.'

Even Toby knew it meant, 'How I hate that kid.'

Understandably, Toby didn't let it worry him. He had more exciting things to think about – like planning the party they were bound to have in his honour any time soon.

And what a party it turned out to be. Nothing less than epic.

APPENDIX
SARIN FACTS

Sarin is a man-made chemical (known as a nerve agent) and one of the most toxic substances ever invented. It was first developed in Germany in 1939 as a pesticide but it was soon mass-produced as as a chemical weapon. It has been used against people in Iraq and probably elsewhere in the Middle East.

Exposure to sarin can cause death in minutes and it is difficult to sense its presence, as it is usually odourless and tasteless. It can be inhaled or absorbed very quickly through the skin. A small dose of liquid sarin on the skin (only 0.5 milligrams or the size of a grain of rice) is enough to kill a human in minutes.

Terrorists have used sarin to attack the public. In 1994, a cult called the Aum Supreme Truth released sarin from a truck in the streets of Japan. Several people died and hundreds became sick and needed hospital treatment. In 1995, the same cult took plastic bags filled with liquid sarin into the Tokyo subway system. The terrorists pierced the bags with pointed umbrellas, releasing sarin gas in underground trains and tunnels. Twelve people were killed and over 5,000 were injured. The terrorists were eventually caught, although the last member of the gang took 17 years to be arrested. In 2015 Katsuya Takahashi was finally sentenced to life imprisonment. The terrorists' plot to get their own way through terror failed.

John Townsend was born in Chelmsford, Essex, and discovered his enchantment with books at an early age. As a child, he wrote mini-dramas, silly poems and stories to tell the cat. Whether or not the cat wanted to hear them is another matter!

His love of hiking and the outdoors led him to become a geography teacher in Gloucestershire, writing pantomimes and plays for the annual drama productions. His first publication was inspired by his rusty old Morris Minor and, 200 books later, he is now a full-time writer.